East
Renfrewshire
COUNCIL

Return this item by
the last date shown.

Items may be renewed
by telephone or at
www.eastrenfrewshire.gov.uk/libraries

First published in 2008
by Wayland

This paperback edition published in 2009

Text copyright © Anne Cassidy 2008
Illustration copyright © Martin Remphry 2008

Wayland
338 Euston Road
London NW1 3BH

Wayland Australia
Level 17/207 Kent Street
Sydney, NSW 2000

Series Editor: Louise John
Cover design: Paul Cherrill
Design: D.R.ink
Consultants: Shirley Bickler

A CIP catalogue record for this book is available from the British Library.

ISBN 9780750251877 (hbk)
ISBN 9780750251884 (pbk)

Printed in China

Wayland is a division of Hachette Children's Books,
an Hachette Livre UK Company

www.hachettelivre.co.uk

Wizard Woof

Written by Anne Cassidy
Illustrated by Martin Remphry

WAYLAND

Wizzle the wizard was trying out
a new spell.

"This chicken will lay a golden egg!"
he said.

Wizzle threw gold dust onto the chicken. The chicken squawked and flapped her wings.

Wanda, who was Wizzle's sister,
picked up the chicken. There were
three fluffy chicks underneath,
but no golden egg.

The king hurried into Wizzle's
magic chamber.

"Leave that now," he said.
"Something's wrong with Woof!"

"He just lies in his basket all day. He won't chase the queen's cat or bury any bones, and when I throw a stick, he won't fetch it!" the king said.

"Maybe I could help to cheer Woof up," said Wizzle.

Wizzle looked in his spell book.
"I know just the right spell," he said.

He took out a silk scarf and threw it in the air. A beautiful dragon appeared, blowing fire from its nose.

Woof just closed his eyes and went to sleep.

Wizzle found a different spell book. "This time I'll get the right spell," he said. He mixed together some fizzing moon dust and three drops of magic snake oil.

Suddenly, hundreds of monkeys
began to dance around the room.
Woof put his paws over his eyes.

Wanda sighed and went to fetch a
jar of Wizzle's magic stones. Wizzle
threw some into the air.

He whispered some magic words.
"Izzle, Wizzle, Woo!"

A baby elephant appeared, riding a bicycle! Woof crawled under the throne.

"This is no good!" the king shouted to Wizzle. "Your spells don't work! You're a terrible wizard!"

The king called for the guards.
"Put him in chains and throw him
outside!" he yelled.

Wanda leaned out of the window
and called to Wizzle.

"Don't worry, I'll think of a way to get you back into the castle!" she shouted.

Wanda went for a walk so she could think.

Suddenly, she saw something moving in the bushes.

It was a small hairy dog! The dog
was all alone and looked very sad.

Wanda picked up the little dog and stroked his fur.

She thought about the king's dog, Woof. He was all alone, too.

"I've got a great idea!" she shouted, and ran to see the king.

"Please give Wizzle one last chance," Wanda said. "Please."

So, Wizzle came back to see the king.
"Bring me my magic box!" he said
to Wanda.

Wizzle tapped the box with his
magic wand.

"Izzle, Wizzle, Woo!" he shouted
once again. There was a bark.
Woof sat up and pricked his ears.

Wizzle tapped the box again. The barking got louder and louder!

Woof stood up and began to wag his tail. Wizzle opened the magic box and inside was the small hairy dog.

Woof jumped up onto the queen's lap in excitement. He ran round and round the thrones. He barked and wagged his tail.

The king smiled. "Maybe you're not such a bad wizard after all," he said to Wizzle.

START READING is a series of highly enjoyable books for beginner readers. They have been carefully graded to match the Book Bands widely used in schools. This enables readers to be sure they choose books that match their own reading ability.

The Bands are:

| Pink / Band 1 |
| Red / Band 2 |
| Yellow / Band 3 |
| Blue / Band 4 |
| Green / Band 5 |
| Orange / Band 6 |
| Turquoise / Band 7 |
| Purple / Band 8 |
| Gold / Band 9 |

START READING books can be read independently or shared with an adult. They promote the enjoyment of reading through satisfying stories supported by fun illustrations.

Anne Cassidy has written lots of books for children. Many of them are about talking animals who get into trouble. She has two dogs, Charlie and Dave, but, sadly, neither of them talk to her! This time she wanted to write about a funny wizard who gets his spells mixed up.

Martin Remphry grew up on the tiny Channel Island of Sark. He has always loved drawing, especially spooky things such as witches and wizards, so it was a dream come true for him to illustrate Wizzle. He loves the funny ingredients Wizzle uses for his spells, even if they don't always work as he hopes!